W9-CSZ-387

THE NATURE OF LONGING

Winner of the Flannery O'Connor Award for Short Fiction